A City Under the Sea

A City Under the Sea

Life in a Coral Reef

by Norbert Wu

Atheneum Books for Young Readers

*F*or Peter Brueggeman,
a good friend and diving buddy

All of the photographs in this book were made possible
by the generosity of diving operations throughout the
world. Thanks goes to the crew and staff of Borneo
Divers; Doris Welsh of Galapagos Network; the *Dream
Too* in the Bahamas; Captain Morgan's Resort in Belize;
the *Okeanos Aggressor* in Costa Rica; Dive Taveuni, Ocean
Pacific Club, and Sea Fiji in Fiji; the *Galapagos Aggressor*
and *Eric* in the Galapagos; the *Ghazala II* and the *Perla* in
the Red Sea; the *Isla Mia*, Anthony's Key Resort, and the
Institute for Marine Sciences in Roatan, Honduras; the
Caribbean Explorer in Saba; the *Ambar III* in the Sea of
Cortez; Seychelles Underwater Center in the Seychelles
Islands; and the *Fantasea* in Thailand. My family has
been the best, and without helpers like Kris Ingram, I
wouldn't be able to do what I do best.

Atheneum Books for Young Readers

An imprint of Simon & Schuster Children's Publishing Division

1230 Avenue of the Americas

New York, New York   10020

Text and photographs copyright © 1996 by Norbert Wu

All rights reserved including the right of reproduction

in whole or in part in any form.

Designed by Eileen Rosenthal

The text of this book is set in Berkeley Oldstyle

Printed in the United States of America

First Edition

10 9 8 7 6 5 4 3 2 1

ISBN 0-689-31896-0

Library of Congress Catalog Card Number 95-78733

*Half title: Caesar grunts; title page: clownfish with a giant
anemone, sea fan polyps; copyright page: anemonefish*

Introduction: The Open Ocean

In the clear, warm waters of the open ocean, an old green sea turtle makes her way to the surface. She pokes her head above the water to breathe and to look around. All around her, for miles and miles, stretches the deep blue of the open ocean. A human would be utterly lost in this endless sea without the proper instruments. But this turtle, like all sea turtles, knows her way through earth's vast oceans, and she slips beneath the water, again taking up the slow, powerful strokes that will eventually bring her to the island of her birth. The turtle disappears again into the blue, passing through shifting rays of sunlight that dance down to the dark, bottomless depths below.

Scientists have long marvelled at how sea turtles can find their way through hundreds of miles of ocean to the beach where they were born. No one knows how the sea turtles do it. They might be able to find their way home by detecting the stars, currents, gravity changes, smells, or things that scientists haven't discovered yet.

The Coral Atoll

After days and days of swimming, the green sea turtle approaches the island of her birth. This island is a coral atoll, an undersea mountain that rises straight up from the ocean bottom 2,000 feet below. The island itself started life millions of years ago as an undersea volcano, which erupted to form a cone above the water. As the volcano grew older, it sank slowly below the water. The corals grew on the shallow sides of the sinking volcano, forming a ring of corals that surrounds an inner lagoon, the crater of the old volcano. At one end of this lagoon lies the beach where the turtle was born; at the other end is the lagoon pass, where it opens to the sea. At certain times of the day, the

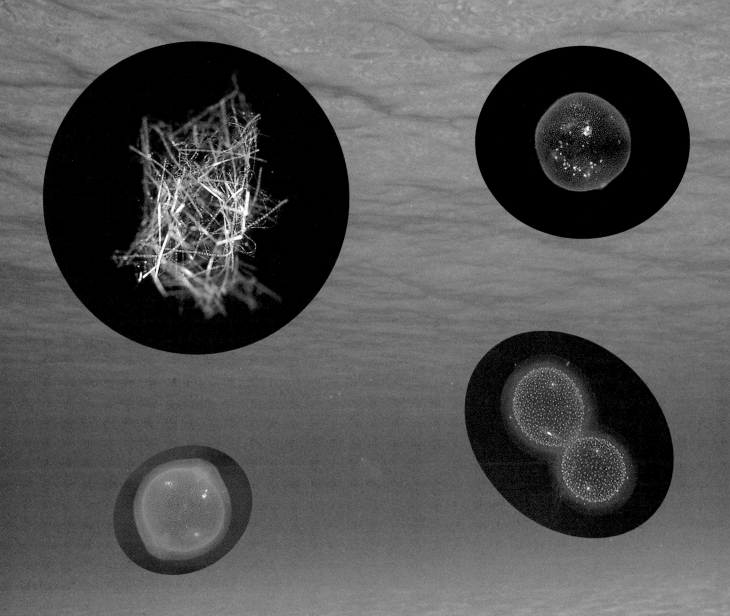

outgoing tides create a strong current of water that pulls the warm, shallow waters of the lagoon out to sea. This water is filled with plankton, tiny plants and animals that are too small to see. In places like the shallow lagoon, the plankton grows so quickly, it turns the water cloudy.

3

Whale shark

The Lagoon Pass

All sorts of large animals gather near the lagoon pass to feed on the plankton-filled waters. A whale shark, the largest fish in the ocean, glides by, mouth open. Although whale sharks are huge, they are not dangerous to the turtle, because they feed by straining plankton from the water. The gills inside their huge mouths act as strainers, which filter the plankton from the shark's big gulps of water.

Swooping and gliding, what look like flying blankets swim through the lagoon

4

Manta rays and hammerhead sharks

pass. These are giant manta rays, fish closely related to sharks. Like the whale shark, manta rays are filter feeders. They also live by straining the plankton from the rich seawater.

Other sharks gather near the pass also. A school of nearly two hundred hammerhead sharks circles the atoll endlessly, almost blocking out the sun with their bodies. Their eyes are on the end of their strange hammer-shaped heads. Scientists think that the shark's hammerhead allows it to make better uses of its senses of smell and sight.

In the distance, a magnificent fish swims with a quick burst of its tail.

This is a sailfish, a speedy, streamlined swimmer with a long bill that looks like a sword, and a dorsal fin that it raises to resemble a sail when it is threatened.

The old turtle has seen all of these creatures of the open ocean before. As a small juvenile, she had to take great care to escape the notice of the sailfish and hammerhead sharks and other creatures of the reef such as groupers and snappers. Now, however, she is so large that none of these animals is a danger. She rises to the surface to take a breath, and she looks over the lagoon to the pink sandy beach that will be her destination tonight. After a moment, she dives down to the sandy bottom by the lagoon pass, to rest while waiting for the tide to change.

The Sand

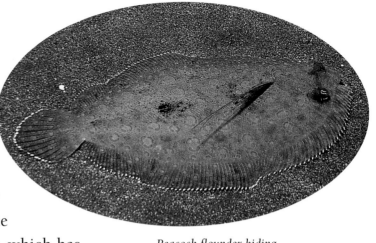

*Peacock flounder hiding
in the sand*

the sandy bottom looks like a huge underwater beach. At first glance, it seems empty, an undersea desert. But a community of animals lives, hunts, and breeds there. The turtle almost lands upon a peacock flounder, which has settled into the sand bottom and covered itself so that only its eyes show. Startled, the flounder bursts out of hiding, narrowly escaping the turtle's landing. It swims away quickly, keeping its two eyes uppermost, wiggling its body in waves. Flounders start out in life looking like normal fish. As they get older and larger, one eye travels over the fish's head, eventually joining the other eye on the right side of the body. Because the flounder can change color to match its surroundings, as it passes from light-colored sand to darker sand, it also becomes darker. Then it finds a small patch of rocks and settles back into the sand among them with only its eyes showing once again.

Garden eels

The large, six-foot long green sea turtle also settles down upon the sand and falls asleep. Slowly, all around her, creatures come out of hiding to resume their activities. A bed of garden eels nearby poke their heads out of their holes, see that the coast is clear, and go back to feeding by plucking food particles out of the water. Eels are long, snakelike fish,

7

A stingray's barbed tail

but these garden eels keep most of their bodies hidden within their burrow, ready to retreat into the sand if an enemy appears. They look like charmed cobras dancing on the sea bottom as they sway to the water currents, plucking out their food.

Close to the sleeping turtle, a large stingray glides by, using its large "wings" (actually flattened pectoral fins) to shake up the sand. It is looking for its favorite food—buried clams. Like the flounder, the stingray is a flat-shaped fish. Its eyes are on top of its body, but its mouth is on the bottom. It has a long tail that has a sharp barb, or spine, in the middle. The stingray uses this tail for defense—it can whip its tail up, stabbing the barb into an enemy. A large triggerfish, shaped like a football, follows the stingray closely, as do silvery jacks and colorful wrasses, all feeding on the worms, small shrimp, and crabs that the ray has unearthed in its search for clams.

Trigger fish

Disturbed by the activity around her, the green sea turtle awakens. She rises up from the sandy sea bottom and slowly, majestically, swims off to the coral wall on the sides of the old crater. As she passes over the bed of garden eels, they disappear into their burrows, re-emerging as soon as she passes, creating a living wave, rippling down the sand as she passes over them.

The Coral Reef

A living coral reef, an immense city under the sea, covers the steep sides of the ancient volcano. Coral reefs are the largest structures ever built by living things. The reefs actually have been created by millions upon millions of tiny coral polyps, animals that grow upon one another in colonies. Corals are invertebrates, animals without backbones. They are shaped like sacs and use stinging tentacles to paralyze their prey and bring it to their stomach. Each coral polyp secretes a limestone skeleton, attached to the skeletons of the polyps around it to hold the city together. Over thousands and thousands of years, these polyps gradually erected the huge, intricate limestone reefs that exist off tropical coasts and islands.

Each colony of corals grows together to form a particular shape, and the sea turtle passes over a number of differently shaped coral colonies. A brain coral forms a large

Above, coral polyps emerge at night. Below, a blue chromis swims over brain coral.

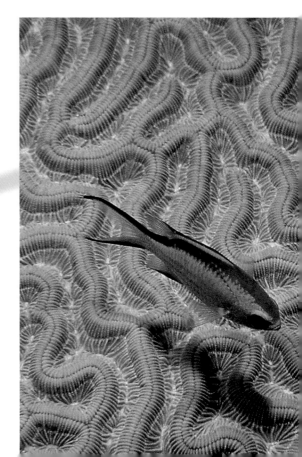

round colony, grooved and shaped like a brain. A large bed of lettuce coral rises from the reef wall, and a cabbage coral colony grows right beside it. A huge stand of staghorn coral grows at the top of the reef wall, covering it with thousands of fingerlike branches. Mustard-colored fire coral covers dead sea fans and dead coral heads. Fire coral is named because of the intense burning sensation that it causes on contact with human skin.

The corals grow so tightly together, in such wild profusion of shapes and sizes, that the turtle can't find a place to settle down. She continues swimming along the reef, looking for a crevice where she can find some peace and quiet. All around her is the hustle and bustle of this undersea city.

Clockwise from left, fire coral; fairy basslets and lettuce coral; sea turtle rests on staghorn coral

Cleaner wrasse and angelfish

The Cleaning Station

like a city, the coral reef has places to live, to socialize, and even to get haircuts and manicures. One large brain coral head is alive with activity. Several different kinds of fishes are lined up around the coral, and at the center, a scribble-faced angelfish hovers head-down, shivering as a pair of tiny, neon-colored cleaning wrasses pass over its body, into its mouth, and out through its gills. This is a cleaning station, the combination barbershop and manicure shop of the coral reef. The cleaning wrasses display their neon colors to attract their customers—larger fish of all kinds. When a customer comes to the cleaning station, it holds still, allowing the cleaning wrasses to go all over its body, cleaning it of parasites and dead skin. The wrasses get a free meal, and the customers are kept clean and parasite-free. Without these cleaning stations, the fishes of the coral reef would become overridden with parasites and die. Customers include fishes like the brightly-colored coral groupers and moray eels, which, under other circumstances, would snap up tasty morsels like these wrasses in an instant.

Batfish being cleaned

The cleaning stations are everywhere in the reef. In a coral cave, a pair of moray eels is being cleaned by a barberpole shrimp. When the shrimp has finished with the moray eels, it walks to the top of the coral head and dances along the top. This peculiar dance serves to attract other customers. In a sandy patch by the coral head, a group of batfish wait in line for a cleaning wrasse to finish with its present client. Even such fearsome predators as lizardfish and white tip reef sharks are being cleaned at different places around the reef.

One fish, the sabertooth blenny or false cleaner blenny, looks very much like a cleaning wrasse. It takes up a position near a cleaning station. When it sees a moray eel being cleaned, the blenny quickly darts down and takes a bite out of it. The moray flinches in pain and backs into its hole while the sabertooth blenny darts away in search of another victim. This blenny is a mimic, a fish that resembles another kind of fish. It uses its resemblance to the cleaning wrasse to get a free meal without giving a service in exchange.

Left, a barberpole shrimp and moray eels. Below, a lizardfish and cleaner wrasse

symbiosis

The cleaning station is an example of symbiosis, a relationship between two different types of animals that helps both. The creatures of the reef take part in many of these relationships. In fact, the entire community of the coral reef depends on animals working together in these symbiotic, mutually beneficial ways.

The coral polyps themselves get much of their food from plants, a type of algae called zooxanthellae, that live in their bodies! These tiny plants, found within the coral polyp, create food using the energy of the sun in a process called photosynthesis. The corals live partially on the sugars and starch produced by the algae, and the plants get nourishing gases and essential nutrients from the waste products of the coral. The corals supplement their diet by capturing small prey from the plankton, and the nutrients from the prey are cycled back and forth between corals and their zooxanthellae. Even giant clams have zooxanthellae within their bodies.

The green sea turtle has finally found a place to rest, a ledge under a coral bommie—a large outcropping of the reef. On the edge of the ledge is a sea anemone, a creature that resembles a big flower. Sea anemones are also invertebrates, and they are closely related to corals. They have a big muscular foot, stinging tentacles on top of the foot, and a mouth in the middle of the tentacles. Unlike corals, however, anemones do not secrete a hard limestone skeleton and they do not gather in

Anemonefish among tentacles of anemones

colonies. Like corals, they use their stinging tentacles to catch planktonic prey, and they may even catch animals as large as fish, crabs, and sea stars. Anemones come in all colors of the rainbow, and they live in almost every place that they can hold onto with their strong foot.

Swimming all around and even within the anemone is a family of anemonefish, or clown-fish. These brightly colored fish spend nearly their entire lives within a host anemone, pro-tected by the anemone's stinging tentacles. They hover within the anemone whenever they are threatened. Anemonefish are not actually immune to the anemone's sting, but when they are juveniles, these small fish pick out a host anemone and repeatedly brush up and wriggle against the stinging tentacles. Gradually the anemonefish become familiar to their host and are able to dart right into the ring of tentacles without harm. In exchange, the anemonefish clean the anemone of debris, and they may even lure in other fish for the anemone to trap and eat.

The two largest anemonefish are a pair—male and female. The smaller male is in a constant state of nervousness and activity. He nips and tugs at the anemone, trying to make it spread out, so that it covers the nest of orange eggs that he is tending at its base. The male

14

Anemonefish guards its eggs

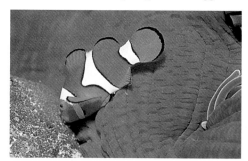

checks on the nest constantly, blowing water over the eggs to keep them fresh, and making sure that the anemone's tentacles protect the eggs from other hungry fishes. When the eggs hatch, the tiny babies, or fry, will become part of the plankton, drifting along with the ocean's currents. After a few weeks, juveniles that have survived will settle down onto another coral reef, with a new host anemone.

Other anemones around the reef have other inhabitants. One bright pink anemone shelters a cleaning shrimp, which dances and waves its antennae. A pair of porcelain crabs sits within a large carpet anemone, which has short, stubby tentacles and is spread over a wide area of the reef. The crabs are filter-feeding, using finely branched mouthparts to strain food particles out of the water.

In the sand on the ledge, a hermit crab lumbers by. Hermit crabs protect their soft bodies by living in old shells of any shape that will fit them. As an additional protection, this hermit crab carries a pair of anemones around with it on its shell! When the hermit crabs finds another empty shell that it likes better, it will move to the new shell, then gently stroke the anemones until they move over to the new shell, too!

Cleaner shrimp (background) and porcelain crabs (top right) in anemones. A hermit crab (bottom right) carries anemones on its shell

15

Life Within Life

Waking up, the green sea turtle blinks and decides to make her way to the surface. It is midday, and she looks over the route she must take tonight to get to the beach: over the coral wall to the reef crest, into the shallow lagoon, and finally to the beach. Taking slow, deep breaths at the surface, she picks out a shady spot above the beach, under a pair of pandalus trees, where her eggs will be kept dry and warm, but not too hot. Ever patient, she drops back below the surface, back down to the reef below. She follows a current that sweeps her along the coral wall.

The sea turtle passes brightly colored soft corals and sea fans growing from the wall. Soft corals are colonies of corals that do not have hard skeletons. They inflate with water during times of current, feeding on food particles that they catch. Sea fans, which look like flattened bushes, are actually colonies

From top to bottom, sea fans and soft corals; long-nosed hawkfish; cowrie snail on soft coral; a school of fairy basslets

of animals. The fans usually grow so that they face right into the current. This way the polyps that make up the fan can filter through as much water as they can for food. Soft corals and sea fans come in many different colors, and they provide shelter and protection for another entire community of animals. Though at first glance, a large sea fan appears empty, closer inspection reveals that it is home to a number of animals. Gobies and blennies—tiny fish—dart about the fans, as do long-nosed hawk-fish. Small cowries, snails with a shell, live on the soft corals and sea fans as well, their colors matching the colors of their host.

The current that passes along the coral wall is like a wind that brings food particles—the plankton. In fact, the entire reef community lives in one way or another by trapping plankton for food.

Huge schools of fairy basslets swim out from the reef wall, creating a wave of color. These tiny, brightly colored fish leave the protection of the reef to feed, then all dart back at once at the first sign of danger.

The sea turtle rides with the current for a short way, then settles for another nap inside the large

17

Hawksbill turtle in a giant barrel sponge

opening of a giant barrel sponge. Sponges, colonial animals like sea fans and corals, also feed on tiny food particles filtered from the water.

Along the tops of many sea fans are clusters of bright, feathery animals that look like flowers or dust mops. These are called feather stars or crinoids. Crinoids climb to the tops of sea fans and coral heads in order to reach the best current, and the most food. They are really a type of sea star, and like all sea stars, they have many arms that all come together to a central disk. Crinoids' long arms are lined with sticky, feather-like fingers. They wave their long, sticky arms about in the current to catch food particles. The fingers then hand the particles over, finger by finger, down to the central disk, where the crinoid's stomach is located.

Even a small animal like the crinoid hosts a community of creatures within the shelter of its body. These animals that live within other, larger animals are engaged in another type of relationship, called commensalism. A commensal shrimp lives within the arms of a crinoid, and while it obtains protection from the crinoid and may steal food from the crinoid's arms, it does not harm it. A pair of clingfish also swim about and within the crinoid's waving arms, and a small crab, colored just like the yellow crinoid, waves its claws out from under the crinoid's feet, hoping to grab a particle of food.

Crinoid on sea fan

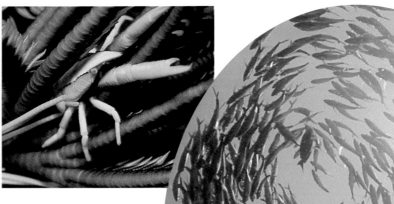

Above, a clingfish and a crab hide in criniods.
Right, jacks circling. Below, parrotfish.

Bright, colorful fish swim all around
the reef, going about their daily business.
Above the turtle, a school of silvery jacks
circles in an endless dance. Off the wall,
barely visible in the distance, a school of
hundreds of barracuda swim in formation.
Within the reef itself, it seems that all the animals
of the earth have been transformed into strange fish
that have their names. Gaudy parrotfish flit among the
reef. They crush the limestone skeletons of the coral with their beak-like mouths,

creating sand as they feed on the polyps. A lionfish sits
among a school of cardinalfish, waiting for a chance to
gulp down an unwitting prey. When a lionfish is hunt-
ing, it mutes its colors and tucks in its fins, to blend
into the background. When it is alarmed by an enemy,
however, it spreads out its fins and brightens its colors
to show its stripes. The lionfish advertises its venomous
spines this way, warning off any potential enemies.
    Cowfish putter about the reef, scorpionfish and

19

Above left to right, scorpionfish; leaf fish; sea horse. Left, lionfish. Below left, cowfish. Below right, trumpetfish

frogfish sit motionless in wait for ambush, and leaf fish flip and flop in the current, like leaves in a wind. A seahorse, a fish that looks nothing like a fish, uses its tail to hold onto one sea fan. A trumpetfish, long and thin, blends in perfectly with the long branches of another. A porcupinefish hovers nearby, looking like a spiked pincushion. When threatened, it can blow itself up like a balloon. Since it is covered with body armor and spines, the pufferfish swims by fluttering its side (pectoral) fins rather than swishing its tail from side to side like most other fishes.

Butterflyfish of all shapes and colors flit about the reef. One pair of spotfin butterflyfish swim together closely for protection. The big spots on their tails, and the line that disguises their eyes, may fool predators. If a predator tries to attack the butterflyfish, it may go for the spot on the tail instead of the real head. As they swim together, the spots on the two butterflyfishes' tails may look like the two eyes of a much larger fish. Angelfish, in their bright colors, also roam the reef. The angelfish and

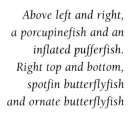

butterflyfish are often seen in pairs, but rarely are more than two of the same kind seen together. Both angelfish and butterflyfish divide the reef into territories that they defend against intruders of the same species. Scientists have discovered that each species of butterflyfish feeds on different algae, corals, or other food on the reef. A different species entering the territory doesn't present competition for food. But if another of the same kind comes in, the butterflyfish will chase it away.

Above left and right, a porcupinefish and an inflated pufferfish. Right top and bottom, spotfin butterflyfish and ornate butterflyfish

Several types of angelfish may have juveniles that look the same, even though the adults look very different. The adults give the juveniles a break when they are growing up. Often, the juveniles are cleaners, sporting bright colors that identify them as such. Because the juveniles are not eating the same foods as the adults, they are allowed to stay within a territory. As the juveniles get older and begin to take on adult colors, the adults will chase them away.

A long-nosed butterflyfish has discovered a crown-of-thorns starfish feasting on a coral head. Like all sea stars, the crown-of-thorns feeds by throwing its stomach out of its body, to cover its prey. The butterflyfish nips at some of the sea star's tube feet, and the crown-of-thorns moves off. It leaves behind dead coral, bleached white because it has eaten the polyps, leaving only a coral skeleton.

As the crown-of-thorns moves across the reef, its trail is picked up by a Triton's trumpet snail. This large snail likes to eat crown-of-thorns sea stars, and when it finally catches up to the sea star a few minutes later, it makes quick work of it.

Left and above, crown-of-thorns starfish feed on coral.
Center, Triton's trumpet snail

Coral reefs are very fragile. Coral polyps are easily killed by water that is too warm, by population explosions of predators like the crown-of-thorns, by diseases that suddenly show up, and by sediment such as sand, mud, or a cover of branches. Often, man's development around coastlines has killed entire coral reefs. Hotels built near a coral reef might discharge sewage or change the flow of currents near a reef, killing it with sediment. Pollution might cause a crown-of-thorns population explosion. Removing Triton's trumpet snails from a reef to collect their pretty shells could also allow crown-of-thorns sea stars to increase in population. Fortunately, this coral atoll is far away from other islands, and people do not live here.

Bleached coral

A school of blue-green chromis

Dusk

As the sun goes down and the waters darken, barracuda and large jacks start patrolling the outer edges of the reef. They are watching the masses of small fish that swim out from the reef's protection to feed on passing food particles. The reef is so jam-packed with these tiny fish that they seem like waves of color flowing around its edges. As each fish in this mass tries to reach a food particle before its neighbor, the wave moves farther and farther from the reef. The predators are watching for a fish that has wandered out too far. A jack sees one and darts in; the wave of fish quickly retreats. At dusk, predators are harder to see, and the entire reef becomes more active with the hunters and the hunted.

On the beach, a nest of green sea turtle eggs has hatched. The hatchlings broke out of their eggs nearly an hour ago, and they have waited for the sun to go down

23

before bursting out of their nest. Unfortunately, the sounds of their struggle have
been heard by many predators, all of whom have been watching for signs of baby
turtles. As the first hatchling emerges from the sand and scrambles madly for the
ocean, it is seen by a mockingbird that darts in and grabs it. Hundreds of hatchlings pour out of the nest, look about in a daze, then madly rush to the surf. A
monitor lizard, flicking its tongue, snatches up a dozen of them. Ghost crabs rise
up out of the sand like apparitions to attack others. Only half of the baby turtles
make it to the water. They swim frantically to the open ocean, and the few lucky
ones that make it past the reef edge without being eaten by sea eagles, swooping
from above, or groupers, swimming from below, will spend the next few days
paddling through the vast ocean to reach the equator.

Night

Tubastrea coral open at night

Once the sun sets, the reef settles down. The fishes of the day find crevices within the coral to sleep. Many turn down their electric bright hues of the day to more muted sleeping colors. A brilliantly colored parrotfish settles down in a coral cave. He spits out a cocoon of mucus that slowly covers his entire body. This cocoon serves to mask his smell to the moray eels that hunt at night.

The entire face of the reef is changing as the coral polyps unfold themselves from their limestone skeletons and extend their tentacles to catch passing food particles in the current. An entirely different community of animals comes out to forage on the reef. Most of these animals hide deep within coral crevices during the day, so that daytime fishes, like that longnose butterflyfish, can't nip off their arms or feet. Crabs, shrimp, and brittle stars come from their daytime hiding places to sit on top of sea fans. A basket star, which has spent the day curled up in a tight ball at the base of a sea fan, unfurls its hundreds of arms, all of which branch into smaller and smaller ones. It clambers to the top, where it

A parrotfish in its mucus net

25

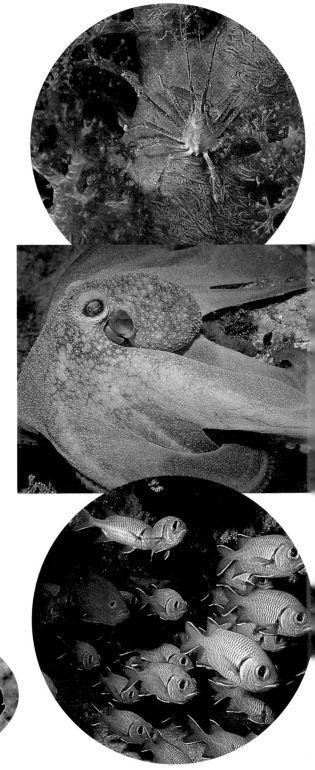

Clockwise from left, decorator crab; spider crab;
octopus; squirrelfish; flashlight fish

will spend the night combing the currents for plankton. A decorator crab, which has covered itself with living sponges, has hidden all day on the rocks below the sea fan. It crawls to the top of another fan, also seeking plankton drifting by in the current.

An octopus emerges from its den and pulsates with excitement as it discovers its favorite food, a clam, buried in the sand. It envelopes the clam with its many arms and carries it back to its den, a hole between two rocks. All around the den are the empty shells of clams that the octopus has feasted on in nights past.

Red squirrelfish and soldierfish come out of their hiding places in caves to search for food. With their large eyes, they can see to hunt by the dim light of the moon. Deeper down the wall, small, bright lights start blinking on and off in coral caves. Soon, one hundred feet down, a great cloud of lights darts about a few yards off the wall.

26

The lights belong to flashlight fish, small fish that have a light organ filled with luminous bacteria underneath each eye. The lights signal to mates and help to attract and pinpoint the planktonic life that the fish eat. Light is flashing everywhere on the reef. A brittle star flashes with green light as it travels over a sea fan. The light is emitted by special cells along the brittle star's arms, called photocytes, and it may cause predators like crabs to avoid the starfish. A shark is enveloped by flashes of light that trace its path through the reef. This light is caused by luminous plankton which fluoresces, or flashes, when disturbed.

The turtle awakens. She makes her way through the nighttime reef, sparkling with light from brittle stars, shrimps, and the phosphorescence of her splashing. She passes over the reef wall, through the breaking surf, and into

Brittle star

the still waters of the lagoon. From here she swims to the pink coral sand and makes her way arduously up the beach. Her size makes it hard for her to move about on land. She is so heavy, her flat shell drags in the sand. The turtle slowly pulls herself along with her flippers, grunting all the while with the strain. She leaves a trail in the sand that looks like tractor wheel marks. After her long trek, she digs a hole and lays her eggs, then she leaves to wander once again through the world's oceans. Her passage back through the reef is marked by a dim glow of phosphorescence, disappearing in her wake.